Leon Spreads His Wings

WENDY LEE

ILLUSTRATED BY

PETR HORÁČEK

WALKER
BOOKS

For Nathan

First published 2008 by Walker Books Ltd
87 Vauxhall Walk, London SE11 5HJ

2 4 6 8 10 9 7 5 3

Text © 2008 Wendy Lee
Illustrations © 2008 Petr Horáček

The right of Wendy Lee and Petr Horáček to be identified as author
and illustrator respectively of this work has been asserted by them in
accordance with the Copyright, Designs and Patents Act 1988

This book has been typeset in Bembo Educational
and NFJoe-ExtraBold

Printed and bound in Great Britain by J.H. Haynes & Co. Ltd

British Library Cataloguing in Publication Data:
a catalogue record for this book is available from the British Library

ISBN 978-1-4063-0715-3

www.walker.co.uk

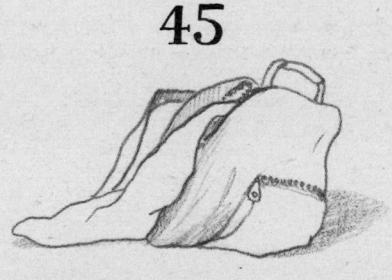

Going on Holiday

Leon's family wanted to go on holiday, but they couldn't decide where.

"Let's vote," said Dad. "We can each say where we want to go, and we'll choose the best idea."

Mum thought that sounded fair. "It will be like when they choose a prime minister," she said.

Leon couldn't
imagine how a holiday
could be like a prime minister,
but he liked having a say.
It made him feel grown up.

Dad went first. "Let's go
to Jamaica," he said.
"Then you can see
where I was born.
It's beautiful."

8

Leon's grandma was always telling
him about life in the Caribbean.

"I've seen a thousand photos
of where you were born,"
he told his dad.
"I don't want to
go to Jamaica."

It was Mum's turn next. "I vote for Egypt," she said. "We can visit the Pyramids and then spend some time on the beach."

"We can look at pictures of the
Pyramids in my book on mummies,"
Leon said, "and there
are beaches here.
I don't want to
go to Egypt."

"It's your turn now," said Dad. "Where do *you* want to go?"

"Actually, I don't mind," replied Leon, "as long as we don't have to get there on a plane. I don't want to fly."

"Aeroplanes are the safest way to travel," said Mum.

"I don't care,"
said Leon stubbornly.
"I don't want
to go on one."

His parents looked at each other and smiled.

"I don't mind not going to Jamaica," said Dad. "August isn't the best time of year in the Caribbean."

"I don't mind not going to Egypt," said Mum. "It can get unbearably hot there."

"I know," said Mum excitedly.
"Let's go on a mystery holiday."

Leon had no idea what that meant.

"We'll pack up the car, take the tent,
then just drive and see where we end
up," she explained.

"Great idea," agreed Dad. "We haven't been camping in years. We'll drive south until we can see the sea."

"And then what?" Leon wanted to know.

"Then we park and the holiday starts," laughed Mum, as though it was obvious.

"Fantastic," said Leon. He was already imagining their tent sitting on a sunny beach. Wouldn't it be great to step out of the tent and into the sea!

19

On their first afternoon at a busy seaside town in the south of England, they decided to explore. "Be nice if there was some sunshine," said Dad, doing up his coat.

"There are chip shops," said Leon, who'd seen lots of them.

On the third day, they walked along the pier for the fourth time.

"There's not really much to do here," said Mum, shaking the raindrops from her umbrella.

Leon was silent.
He didn't want to upset
his mum, but the holiday
was nothing like he'd hoped.
There was a beach, but it had stones
instead of sand. And they hadn't been
able to pitch their tent there anyway,
because they'd had to stay in a place
called a caravan park.

22

And instead
of stepping out
of the door
and into the
sea every morning,
they stepped out of the
door and into the mud.
Leon was glad they hadn't had to fly,
but he did wish they could have gone
somewhere that was sunny all the
time. And had proper sand.

23

Back at school, Leon had to write about his summer holiday. He decided to write about the holiday he wished he'd had. *We went to Jamaica*, he wrote, *where my dad is from. And then to Egypt, where we saw the Pyramids.*

"It sounds like you had a lovely time," said his teacher.

Baby Comes
to Visit

Leon's Auntie Gwen lived in Spain with her husband, Pablo, and their baby, Jorge. Leon had never met Jorge. Auntie Gwen often sent photos by email, so Leon could see that he looked like a lot of fun. He wished they lived nearer.

27

When Mum said "Get in the car" on
the first day of half-term, Leon had no
idea where they were going. "It's a
surprise," was all she would say.

28

"But I haven't even had breakfast,"
said Leon. He liked surprises, but he
liked breakfast too.

Mum handed him some juice and
a banana. Then she put the radio on
and drove.

"How will I know when
we're nearly there?" Leon asked
after about half an hour.
"When you see planes in
the sky, we'll be very close,"
said Mum.

"You tricked me!" cried Leon
as a big aeroplane flew overhead.
"I don't want to fly!" He had to
shout because the plane was so loud.

"Just trust me!" yelled Mum,
parking the car.

As they walked through the big glass doors of the airport, Mum smiled the biggest smile ever.

Leon looked where she was looking
and saw Auntie Gwen coming towards
them, holding baby Jorge!

"We're staying for a week," Auntie
Gwen told Leon as they all climbed
into the car.

Leon was so excited – he was getting
a whole week with baby Jorge!

In his car seat Jorge
was holding on to a blue blanket.
"What's that for?" Leon asked.
"It's Jorge's blanky," said Auntie
Gwen. "It makes him feel happy
and safe."

"It must work," said Leon. "He's
just got off a plane and he isn't
even crying."

Auntie Gwen smiled. "Jorge can do anything as long as he has his blanky."

"I could do with one of those," Leon told her.

"Don't be silly," said Mum. "You're much too big."

"Far too grown up for a blanky," agreed Auntie Gwen.

Over the next few days,
Leon and his family went on lots
of outings with Jorge. At the park
Jorge fell over, and
one hug of his
blanky stopped
him crying.

At the zoo a monkey screeched right
in Jorge's face, which was very scary.
Then Auntie Gwen gave him his blanky
and he calmed down straight away.

When it got dark, Leon would point out of the window and whisper to Jorge, "Look, Jorge – there's the moon." And even though Leon was with him, Jorge always clutched his blanky a little tighter in the darkness.

When Jorge
had to go
home, Leon
was sad all day.

He couldn't bear
to eat lunch, and
after supper he tried to
cheer himself up by drawing
a picture of him
and Jorge
dancing on
a Spanish beach.

40

"That's lovely," said Mum. "Let's stick it on the fridge for Dad to see."

When he went into the kitchen, Leon saw Jorge's blanky lying on the counter.

"Mum!" he called. "Jorge has forgotten his blanky. He won't be able to get on the plane!"

"Jorge has already been on the plane," Mum told him. "He'll be back home in Spain by now."

Leon was horrified. "Please ring and check," he said. Mum smiled as she put the phone down. "Jorge slept all the way home," she said.

"He didn't even notice
his missing blanky.
Auntie Gwen says
you can give it to
him next time
you see him."

At school Leon had to write about
his half-term. *My baby cousin came over
from Spain,* he wrote. *He couldn't do
anything without his blanky.*

"Your cousin sounds very sweet,"
said his teacher.

Leon Thinks
He Can

*A*n invitation had come in the post.

"Auntie Gwen's having a big party for baby Jorge's second birthday, and she wants us all to go," Mum told Leon.

Leon was so excited, he felt like he would burst. But then a thought occurred to him.

"Will the party be in Spain?" he
asked later, already knowing the answer.
"Of course it will," Mum told him.
"We'd have to
go on a plane," said
Leon. "And I don't
want to fly."

48

"Oh," said
Mum, thinking
for a moment.
"Well, how about
you stay here with
Dad, and I go on my
own? I'll email lots of photos.
It'll be almost like you're there."

Leon imagined Jorge's party with
a clown and a big cake shaped like
the moon, and he felt very
sad that he wouldn't
be there. And a bit
jealous that his
mum would.

That night, Leon took Jorge's blanky to bed with him, to remind him of Jorge. Just to see what would happen, Leon slept with his night light off for the first time, and he didn't feel scared at all.

The next day, Leon took the blanky with him to the dentist's. He kept it under his top so the dentist wouldn't see, and when the dentist started examining his teeth, Leon held the blanky tightly and thought of Jorge's little face.

Before Leon knew it, the dentist had finished, and he hadn't cried once.

"I will come to Spain," Leon told
his parents later. "I really should
take Jorge's blanky back."
"That's fantastic!"
said Dad, grinning.

Leon didn't tell them that the blanky
worked for him as well. That he
thought the blanky would help him fly.

Leon got out his rucksack to take to
Spain. He packed his new T-shirt with
the big frog on it, to wear
to the party. He chose
three of his favourite
books to read on
the plane. And on
top of everything,
he put the blanky.

On the train to the airport, Leon read
one of his books.

"Are you really OK?" asked Mum.

"Yes," said Leon.

Walking through the airport, Leon
held his head high.

"Are you sure you're all right?" asked
Dad.

"I'm fine," said Leon.

Going down the tunnel that led
onto the plane, Leon was feeling fine
as he reached into his rucksack.
But something wasn't right.
The blanky wasn't there!
It must have fallen out
on the train when he'd
got his book.

And now the plane
was just a few footsteps away.
Mum and Dad were actually
on board, looking back
at Leon. Waiting for him.

"Is everything OK?" asked Mum.

"Get a move on," said Dad.

"I've got a lovely colouring book for you," said a smiling air hostess.

Leon was furious. A colouring book! At his age!

He took a deep
breath and looked at
his mum and dad.

"I'm six years and
three months old," Leon
announced. "I'm too
old for a colouring book,
and far too old for
a blanky," he said,
thinking of little Jorge
without *his* blanky.

And Leon marched
onto the plane,
smiling bravely.

Jorge's party was brilliant, even
though he didn't have a clown – and
his cake was in the shape of a frog,
just like the one on Leon's
T-shirt.

Leon sent a postcard to his teacher:

Dear Miss Harding,
Aeroplanes are the safest way to travel. I will be coming home on one on Sunday. I can't wait to look out of the window and see the clouds again. It feels magical.

From Leon (Blue Class)

Miss Harding
Village School
Little Monkton
England